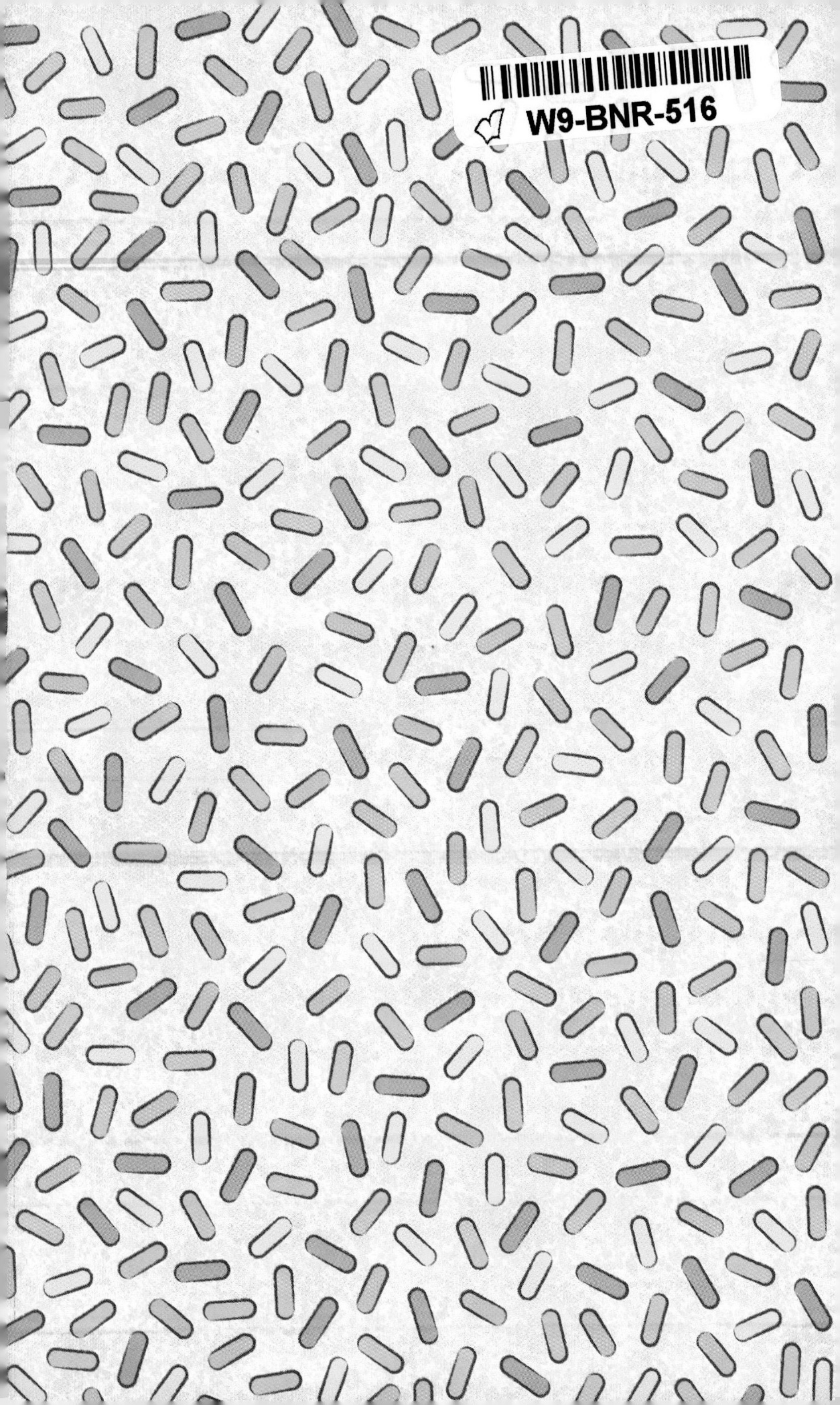

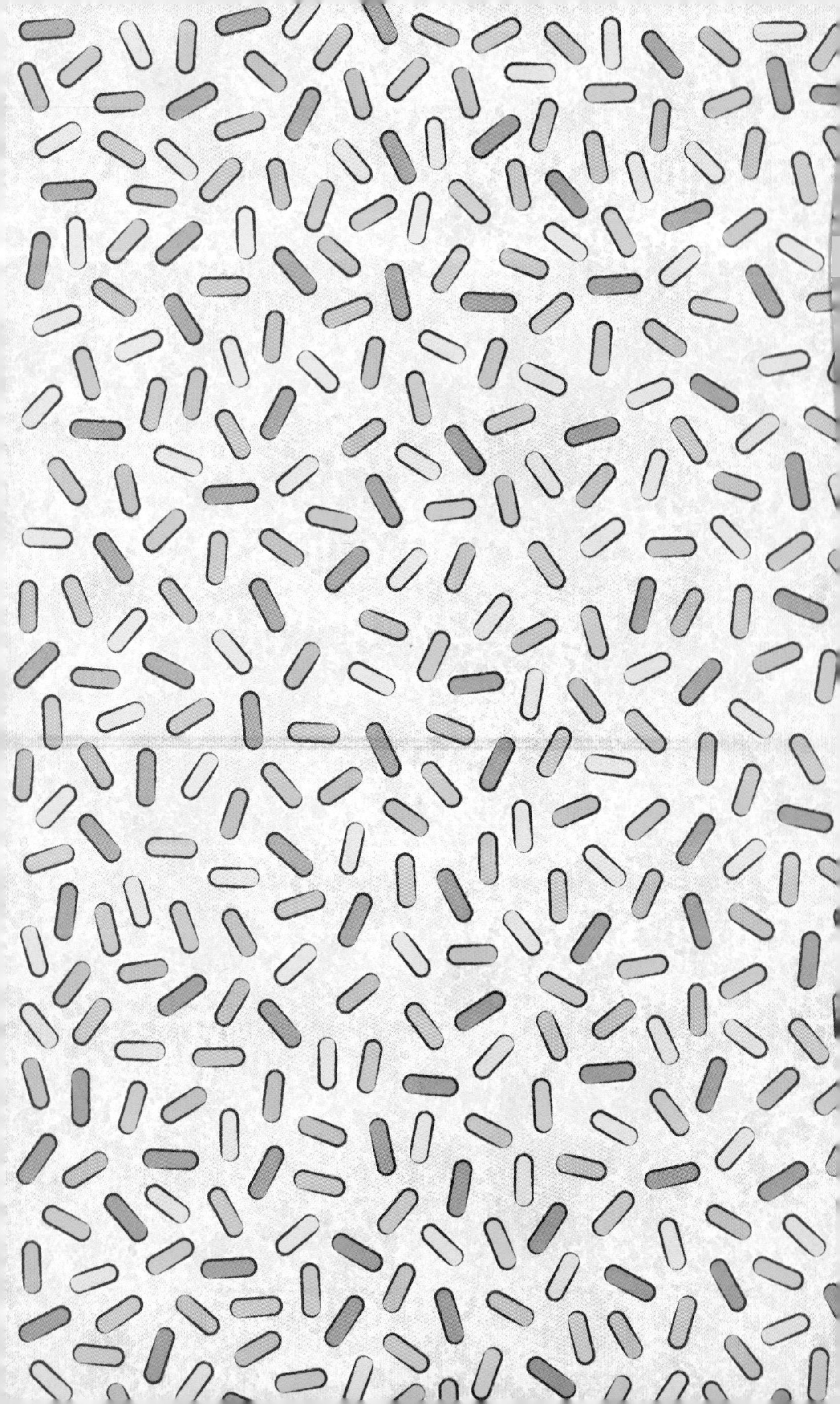

KITTY CONES®
ANYTHING IS PAWS-IBLE!

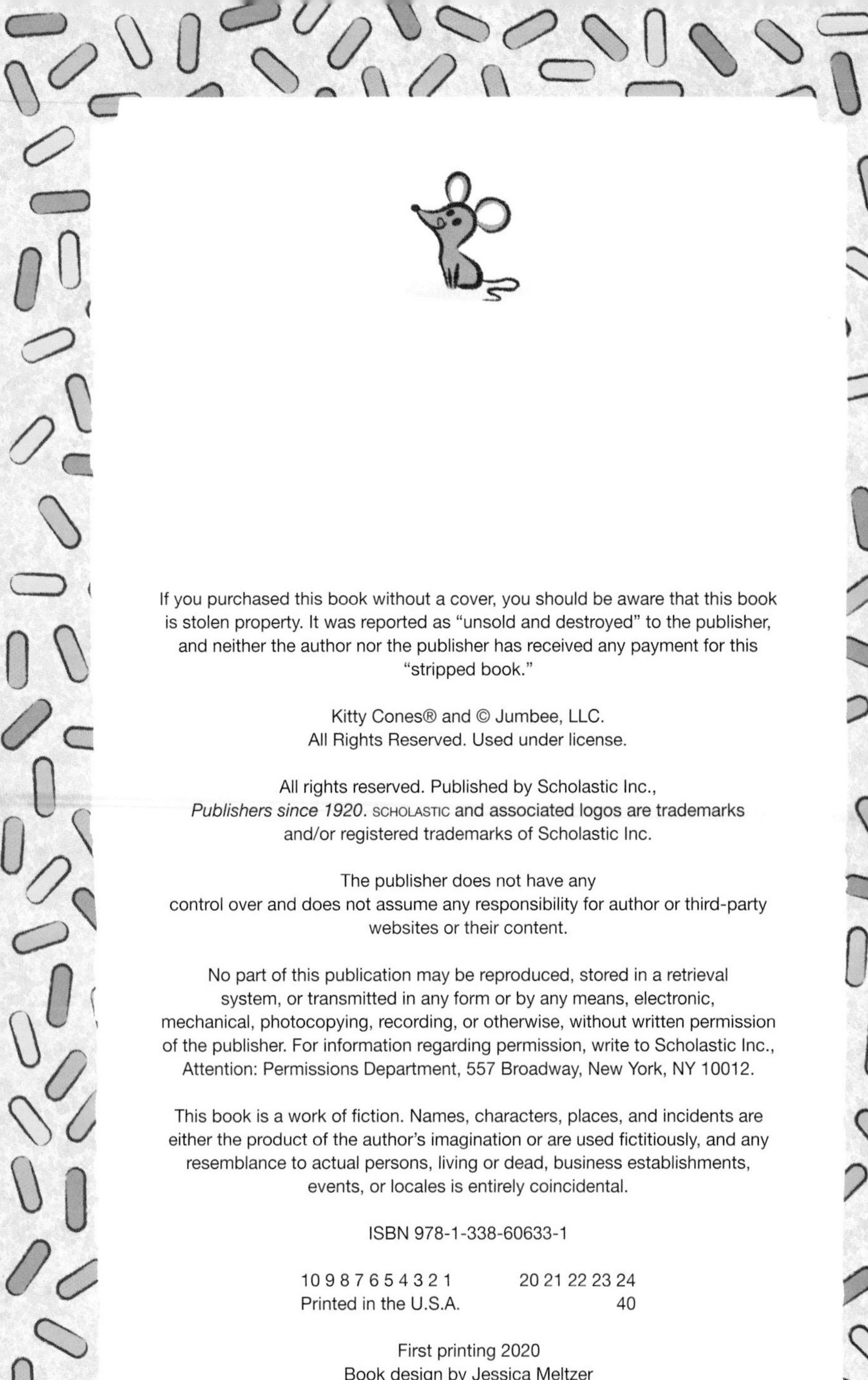

ISBN 978-1-338-60633-1

10 9 8 7 6 5 4 3 2 1 20 21 22 23 24
Printed in the U.S.A. 40

First printing 2020
Book design by Jessica Meltzer

KITTY CONES®
ANYTHING IS PAWS-IBLE!
CREATED BY
RALPH COSENTINO
BY
MEREDITH RUSU
SCHOLASTIC INC.

THE SWEET WORLD OF KITTY CONES

YUMI, **MIYU**, and **KOKO** are three best friends who live in an ice-cream parlor across the bay from **MEW YORK CITY**. These three fluffy friends are *paw*sitively up for adventure so long as they're together! Whether it's fishing for breakfast in the bay, using their cones to launch into space, or building a scratching post as tall as the ***EMPURR* STATE BUILDING**, anything is possible with just a sprinkle of imagination.

Welcome to
Mew York
City
CUTE + CUDDLY + LOVE +
A SCOOP OF FRIENDSHIP
= KITTY CONES!

WELCOME TO MEW YORK CITY

The Kitty Cones' ice-cream purr-lor overlooks Mew York City, the greatest kitty city in the world! There's loads to see and do there, and the Kitty Cones enjoy exploring together.

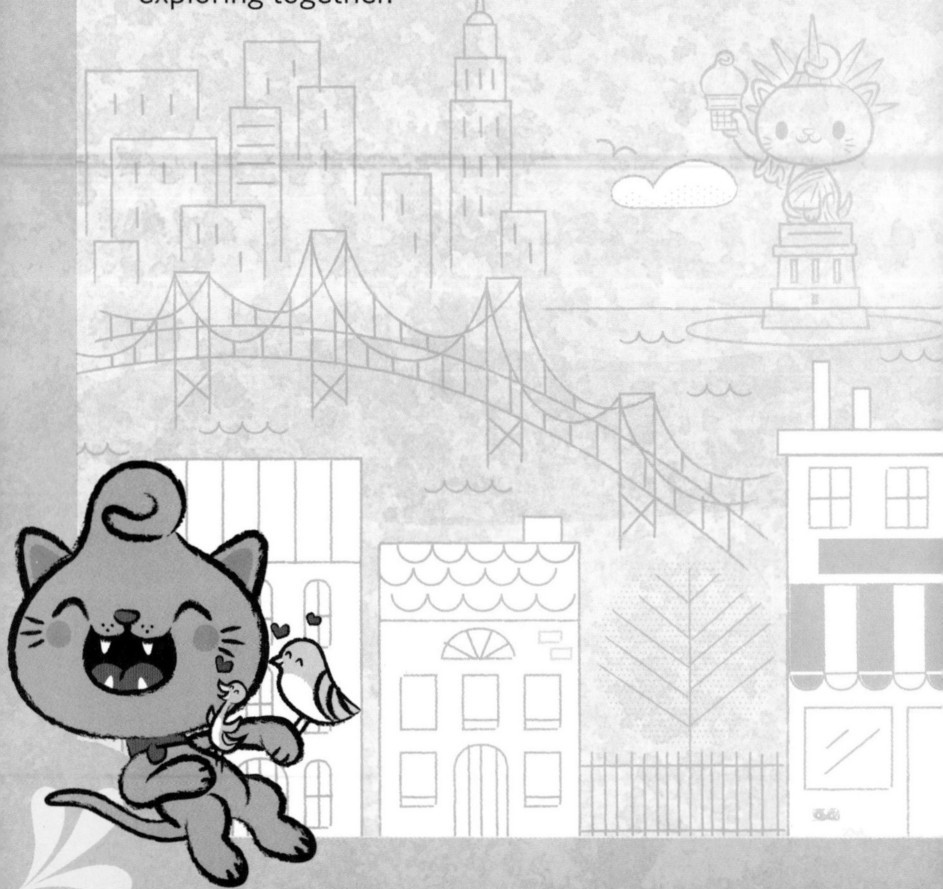

On sunny days, the friends spend the morning chasing birds in **CENTRAL PAWK**. Yumi insists that each new morning will be the day they finally catch those sneaky songbirds and show them that all the Kitty Cones want to do is play!

In the winter, the Kitty Cones go skating at **ROCKERFURLER CENTER**. It's a magical time of year, filled with fur muffs, *tails* of holiday spirit, and twinkling string lights as far as the eye can see.

When summertime rolls around, **CONEY ISLAND** is the place to be. The *Furris* Wheel is always spinning, the sun has everyone *feline* fine, and even though the roller coaster may speed so fast that it causes hair balls, the thrill of the ride is worth it to tell the *tail*.

10 REASONS WHY MEW PURR-SEY IS NOT MEW YORK CITY

The Kitty Cones love **MEW YORK CITY**, but they want to make sure it's never, ever confused for **MEW PURR-SEY**. You see, confusing Mew York City and Mew Purr-sey is just downright wrong. Here's the top ten reasons Mew York City isn't Mew Purr-sey.

I ♥ MEW YORK

1. THE ONLY BUS SYSTEM THAT'S A LITTLE MORE CATTY THAN MEW YORK CITY'S?

   THE MEW PURR-SEY TRAN-*SIT*! THIS BUS SYSTEM GIVES A WHOLE MEW MEANING TO "IF I FITS, I SITS."

2. THE PURR-SEY SHORE IS NICE, BUT ITS BEACH TRAFFIC?

   YOU GOTTA BE *KITTEN* ME!

3. NEW PURR-SEY DOES HAVE SOME GREAT DESTINATIONS, THOUGH,

   LIKE ATLANTIC KITTY, WHERE YOU CAN CURL UP ON THE BEACH WITH SOME MILK AND COOKIES.

4. AND DON'T GET US STARTED ON THE CAPE MEWY LIGHTHOUSE!

IT'S MIYU'S FAVORITE PLACE TO BE!

5. THE BEST PART OF PURR-SEY CITY?

YOU CAN SEE THE WHOLE MEW YORK CITY SKYLINE!

6. BUT YOU DON'T WANT TO SIT IN THE LIN-*CONE* TUNNEL DURING RUSH HOUR.

TRUST THE KITTY CONES ON THIS ONE. IT'S NOT A SWEET TREAT!

7. MEW PURR-SEY HAS THE LARGEST NUMBER OF DINERS IN THE WORLD—

MEANING IT'S GOT THE MOST MILKSHAKES AND ICE-CREAM SCOOPS PER *CAT*-ITA!

8. ANNE CAT-HAWAY, FUR-ANK SINATRA, AND JOHN TAIL-VOLTA

ALL COME FROM MEW PURR-SEY.

9. BUT THE PIZZA AND BAGELS IN MEW PURR-SEY?

TALK ABOUT *HISS*-TERICAL!

10. MEW PURR-SEY IS A VERY NICE PLACE TO VISIT, MAYBE FOR A DAY OR TWO. BUT AS THE KITTY CONES SAY,

IT JUST ISN'T MEW YORK!

10 THINGS ABOUT

1. YUMI, MIYU, AND KOKO HAVE BEEN BEST FRIENDS *FUR*-EVER.

2. THEY LOVE ADVENTURE ALMOST AS MUCH AS THEY LOVE ICE-CREAM.

3. WITH THEIR CONES THEY CAN SAIL, FLY, SLIDE DOWN RAINBOWS, AND EVEN LAUNCH INTO SPACE!

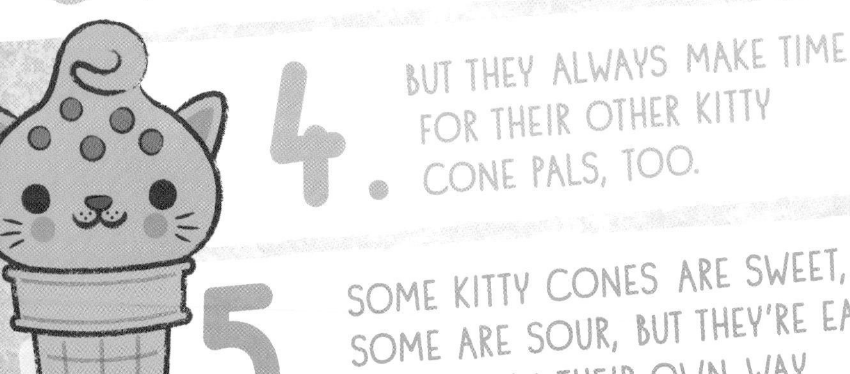

4. BUT THEY ALWAYS MAKE TIME FOR THEIR OTHER KITTY CONE PALS, TOO.

5. SOME KITTY CONES ARE SWEET, SOME ARE SOUR, BUT THEY'RE EACH *PURR*FECT IN THEIR OWN WAY.

TO KNOW KITTY CONES

6. KITTY CONES ENJOY *KITTEN* AROUND WITH THEIR FRIENDS.

7. AND LIVING IN THE HERE AND *MEOW*.

8. EVERYTHING IS BETTER WITH SPRINKLES.

9. ESPECIALLY ICE-CREAM. (*FUR* SURE)

10. THEY KNOW ANYTHING IS *PAWS*-IBLE AS LONG AS THEY'RE TOGETHER.

MEET THE KITTY CONES

YUMI

Yumi has been leaping into adventure and landing on her feet ever since she was a little fluffball! She's a natural leader with dreams as big as a triple-scoop sundae, and while her favorite ice-cream flavor might be vanilla, there's nothing plain about her. Her idea of a *purr*fect day involves chasing rainbows, *cat*-ching up on the daily Mew York City news, and dancing to **TAIL-OR SWIFT'S** new beats at a sweet **PAWJAMA PARTY** with her friends!

ALL ABOUT YUMI

PERSONALITY: Sweet and reliable

FAVORITE ICE-CREAM FLAVOR: Vanilla

LIKES: Sprinkles on her ice-cream

DISLIKES: Hair balls

SWEETEST MEMORY: Meeting her *fur*-ever friends, Miyu and Koko, at the ice-cream *Purr*-lor

CRAZIEST ADVENTURE: Using her cone to rocket past the Milky Way!

HER FRIENDS KNOW: She can be a bit bossy, but on the inside she's a total softie.

MOTTO:

"LET'S TAKE A SCOOP OUT OF LIFE!"

YUMI SAYS . . .

LIFE IS AS COOL AS YOU MAKE IT!

THE ONLY WAY TO FIND A POT OF GOLD IS TO FIRST CHASE THE RAINBOW.

KOKO

Fabulously **FUNNY** and friendly, Koko can't get enough of the sweeter things in life. He races each morning to the playground to go down the slides before the morning dew has worn off. (Instant water slide!) And he's always got a new **MAGIC** trick up his sleeve to impress his friends. (His classic is pulling a rabbit out of a cone.) Koko's friends know they can count on him to bring a smile to their faces. As Koko likes to say,

"LAUGHTER IS THE SWEETEST SOUND THERE IS!"

ALL ABOUT KOKO

PERSONALITY: Carefree

FAVORITE ICE-CREAM FLAVOR: Chocolate

LIKES: Riding the Scoop-de-Loop Coaster at Coney Island

DISLIKES: Saunas. He feels like he's melting in there.

BEST MAGIC TRICK: Making a chocolate sundae disappear

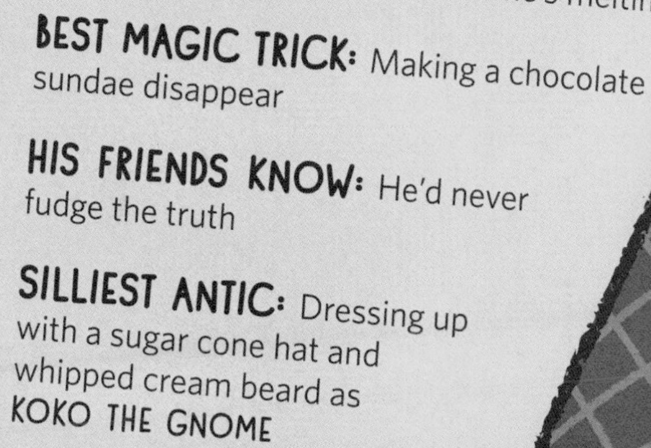

HIS FRIENDS KNOW: He'd never fudge the truth

SILLIEST ANTIC: Dressing up with a sugar cone hat and whipped cream beard as KOKO THE GNOME

SIGNATURE DANCE MOVE: The Coco Loco

KOKO SAYS . . .

WHAT'S LIFE WITHOUT A LITTLE MAGIC?

FRIENDSHIP IS THE CHERRY ON TOP!

MIYU

Adorable little Miyu adores taking cat naps and curling up with the Sundae **MEW YORK TIMES** comics on rainy days. And her absolute favorite thing is playing video games, because she's *berry* good at them! Whether she's building a virtual ice-cream parlor in **MINECAT** or crushing the competition in **CALL OF CUTIE**, her gaming skills are the cat's meow. But no matter what, she's always happy to play with her friends, win or lose. After all, what fun is a game without friends to cheer you on?

ALL ABOUT MIYU

PERSONALITY: Berry Mellow

FAVORITE ICE-CREAM FLAVOR: Strawberry

LIKES: The sound of raindrops on the roof

DISLIKES: Being startled

HAPPIEST MEMORY: The time her friends made her an ice-cream sundae bar to fuel her all-day gaming binge

WOULD NEVER: Gloat over winning

FAVORITE COMIC: *Catman*

CLAIM TO FAME: She entered the *League of Kittens* video game competition at MEW YORK CITY COMIC CONE . . . and won!

MIYU SAYS . . .

THE BEST WAY TO GROW IS TOGETHER!

FRIENDS LIFT YOU UP

SHERBURT

Orange you glad to meet Sherburt? He sure is glad to meet you! Sherburt's personality is as **BRIGHT** as a burst of citrus, and he has a **JUICY SENSE OF HUMOR** to boot. He'll laugh at just about anything, including his own jokes. (Have you heard the one about the cat that ate too much whipped cream? He was coughing up hair balls for days!) The only thing Sherburt loves more than a great joke is the color orange. Rumor has it he once ate a whole box of orange popsicles just to turn his tongue his favorite color.

ALL ABOUT SHERBURT

PERSONALITY: Bright and silly

FAVORITE ICE-CREAM FLAVOR: Orange sorbet

LIKES: Catching the late-night standup act at the Comedy Cone

DISLIKES: Sticky paws

BEST JOKE: What do you call twin Kitty Cones? Cone clones!

FAVORITE TIME OF YEAR: Fall, when pumpkin ice-cream is in season

HIS FRIENDS SAY: Sherburt is a silly kitty!

EARLIEST MEMORY: Frolicking through the orange groves of his farm home as a young kitten

SHERBURT SAYS . . .

LAUGHTER IS THE BEST MEDICINE.

THE BEST SURPRISES POP-UP WHEN YOU LEAST EXPECT THEM!

SOURPUSS

You can pucker up all you want, but Sourpuss isn't one for giving kisses! This **GRUMPY** kitty is quick to poo-poo his friends' grand ideas and tends to sulk around the ice-cream *purr*-lor wondering why everyone else is so cheerful. Still, his friends help him to enjoy the sweeter things in life, like the time they brought him to the lemon tree exhibit at the **MEW YORK BOTANICAL GARDENS**. Ironically, one of Sourpuss's favorite activities is turning lemons into lemonade. Shhh—don't tell him that's the definition of optimism!

ALL ABOUT SOURPUSS

PERSONALITY: Pessimistic

FAVORITE ICE-CREAM FLAVOR: Lemon sorbet

LIKES: Sweet-and-sour candies

DISLIKES: Overly sweet kitties

GETS ANNOYED BY: Surprises. They're fruitless endeavors.

ANSWER TO MOST QUESTIONS: "NOT MEOW."

LITTLE KNOWN FACT: He sleeps with a stuffed kitty named Mr. Squeezes

BIGGEST SECRET: He depends on his friends to add zest to his life

SOURPUSS SAYS . . .

SOMETIMES YOU NEED A LITTLE SQUEEZE OF HOPE.

WHEN LIFE GIVES YOU LEMONS, MAKE LEMONADE!

PURRSTACHIO

There's nothing more soothing than the sound of Purrstachio's **PURR**. That's because this **ZEN KITTY** is all about keeping things *chill*. There's no milkshake machine too loud, dog bark too gruff, or thunderstorm too thundery to startle Purrstachio from her zone. You can usually find her **MEDITATING**. (Rumor has it, her cone will actually levitate.) Just be careful about showing her a bag of catnip. It's her one weakness, and the temptation is enough to make her crack!

ALL ABOUT PURRSTACHIO

PERSONALITY: Purrfectly zen

FAVORITE ICE-CREAM FLAVOR: Pistachio / Green tea

LIKES: Doing yoga in the forest

DISLIKES: Discord

FAVORITE MUSIC: Smoothie jazz

KNOWN FOR: Deep scoops of wisdom

FAVORITE YOGA POSE: Coneward-facing cat

SECRET: One whiff of catnip makes her go nuts!

PURRSTACHIO SAYS . . .

I'M IN THE CONE ZONE.

FRIENDS BRING LIFE BALANCE.

BLACKBARRY

When Blackbarry was just a kitten, he'd spend his days going on imaginary **ADVENTURES** "sailing" the seven C's of the ice-cream parlor (Chocolate, cookie dough, cake batter, cherry, coconut, cheesecake, and cappuccino.) Now, Blackbarry is a full-fledged **BUC-*CAT*-NEER**! Together with his trusty parrot first mate, he sails the true ocean blue in search of golden treasure. He promises the Kitty Cones he'll return to Mew York Bay one day. And when he does, imagine the **LEGEN*DAIRY* *TAILS*** he'll tell!

ALL ABOUT BLACKBARRY

PERSONALITY: Salty

FAVORITE ICE-CREAM FLAVOR: Rum raisin

LIKES: Using his claws to dig for treasure

DISLIKES: Walking the *purr*-lank

GREATEST ADVENTURE: Discovering the legendary temple of the Golden Cone on Dessert Island

FIRST MATE: His parrot, Captain Flint

CATCH PHRASE: "Yo-ho, cookie dough!"

SECRET: Licking an ice-cream cone evenly while wearing an eyepatch is hard.

BLACKBARRY SAYS . . .

FRIENDSHIP BE THE TRUEST TREASURE.

THE LIFE OF A BUC-CAT-NEER IS FULL OF SAARRRRPRISES!

CHIP

Chip is *all* about chocolate chips. He'll put those decadent morsels on anything: ice-cream, pizza, even tuna salad. Maybe it's all the sugar getting to his head, but Chip is always feeling **UPBEAT** and **SPUNKY**. There's no challenge he isn't eager to take on. And he always smells *so* good. He could run a full marathon and still be **MINTY FRESH** at the end of it. No one knows how he does it, but Chip just says he's a "chip off the old block."

ALL ABOUT CHIP

PERSONALITY: Chipper

FAVORITE ICE-CREAM FLAVOR: Mint chocolate chip

LIKES: Collecting mint-condition action cones

DISLIKES: Melted chocolate

HIS FRIENDS SAY: "Chip has a fresh outlook on life."

LITTLE KNOWN FACT: Even Chip's hair balls smell minty fresh.

FAVORITE MEMORY: Baking chocolate-chip cookies with his Grandma Kit

BEST FRIEND: Blackbarry, who always greets him with "Chip, Ahoy!"

CHIP SAYS . . .

WE'RE MINT FOR EACH OTHER.

A LITTLE ENCOURAGE-*MINT* GOES A LONG WAY!

HAYAO

Hayao is originally from **KITTYOTO, JAPAN**. He's a huge **MEOW-NGA FAN**, and is even drawing his own comic series. It's about a group of unsuspecting kitties who are called upon by a superhero named Ha-Meow to save the multiverse using their interdimensional ice-cream cones! Hayao swears his work is completely fictional and that any relation to kitties living or otherwise is purely coincidental. But that seems like only half the true scoop . . .

ALL ABOUT HAYAO

PERSONALITY: Imaginative

FAVORITE ICE-CREAM FLAVOR: Red bean

LIKES: Catnapping and daydreaming

DISLIKES: When the Internet is down

SUPERHERO ALIAS: Ultra Kitty Cone

CLAIM TO FAME: He's a master at *Dance Dance Revomewtion*!

FAVORITE ANIME: *Astro Cat*

CAN USUALLY BE FOUND: Doodling cartoons while basking in the sunlight

HAYAO SAYS . . .

INSPIRATION STRIKES WHEN YOU LEAST EXPECT IT!

ULTRA KITTY CONE TO THE RESCUE!

UMA

Uma is the one and only unicorn Kitty Cone in the world. After a particularly powerful thunderstorm, a giant rainbow appeared over Mew York City, and Uma slid right down! She says she came from a cloud made of **MARSHMALLOW FLUFF**. Although everyone's pretty sure there aren't any other unicorn Kitty Cones out there, she's determined to keep looking for them. It may be a **PIE-IN-THE-SKY DREAM** to find another one, but isn't pie best served à la *meow*?

ALL ABOUT UMA

PERSONALITY: Cheerful and bubbly

FAVORITE ICE-CREAM FLAVOR: Rainbow swirl

LIKES: Shooting stars

DISLIKES: Nay-sayers

KNOWN FOR: Making sprinkles magically sparkle on her ice-cream

PRIZED POSSESSION: A bracelet with charms representing each of her friends

HOBBY: Bedazzling everything like her bedroom, gifts, and cone

BIGGEST DREAM: To find another unicorn Kitty Cone

UMA SAYS . . .

I BELIEVE IN YOU

DREAM BIG
OR GO CONE!

CHIP'S BIG CHALLENGE

A KITTY CONES TAIL

It was a bright, sunny morning in Mew York City. Chip was out for a stroll when, suddenly, *beep beep*! He got a text message from his friend, Yumi, on his iCone.

"Spotted a new ice-cream truck!" Yumi's message read. "Downtown, in the ***FUR*NANCIAL DISTRICT**. Hurry—their special is Triple Dip Mint Chocolate Chip!"

Chip wiggled his whiskers in delight. "Triple Dip Mint Chocolate Chip! That's my favorite!"

Chip hightailed it downtown. He skidded to a stop just outside the World *Fur*nancial Center. Yumi was there, licking a big vanilla ice-cream cone.

"You just missed the truck!" Yumi exclaimed. "The driver headed north on **PAWK AVENUE** toward **KITS BAY**. If you hurry, you can catch it!"

"On my way!" cried Chip. He zoomed off as fast as his paws would carry him. Soon, he spotted his friends Miyu and Sherburt, both holding ice-cream cones of their own.

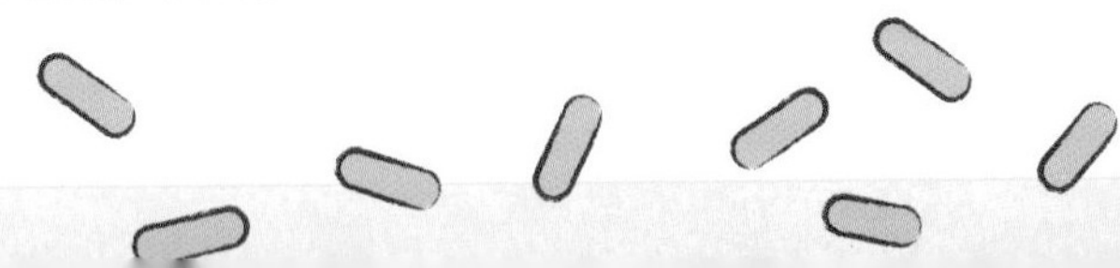

"Are you trying to catch the new ice-cream truck?" Miyu asked. "It headed west toward TRIBECAT."

"Are you kitten me?" Chip asked, out of breath.

"We never joke about ice-cream," said Sherburt. "And you'll *love* this new truck. It's special of the day is . . ."

"Triple Dip Mint Chocolate Chip," Chip exclaimed. "And it's my job to get my paws on those yummy chips! Gotta scat, kitty cats!"

Off Chip ran. He was getting tired, but nothing would dampen his chipper mood when chocolate chips were on the line! When he finally reached Tribecat, he was exhausted. But there, at last, was the new ice-cream truck.

"Hey!" called Chip's friend Hayao. "You're just in time! This new truck's special is . . ."

"Triple Dip Mint Chocolate Chip," Chip panted. "I know. It was almost an im*paw*sible challenge to track it down. But I did it!" Then, Chip turned to the driver. "I'll have a triple-sized Triple Dip Mint Chocolate Chip cone, please."

"Triple-sized?" Hayao asked in surprise. "Isn't that too big?"

Chip smiled. "The bigger the challenge, the bigger the reward."

WHAT KITTY

CONES DO

ICE-CREAM PURR-LOR

ADVENTURE IN EVERY SCOOP

The Kitty Cones may look like normal little kittens, but their adventures are far from ordinary. Using their special cones, they can literally go anywhere and do anything—even blast into outer space! Not every day is worthy of an intergalactic adventure. (After all, why let a warm ray of sunshine purr-fect for a cat nap go to waste?) But whether they're using their cones to climb **MOUNT KITTYMANJARO** or to make a pyramid to cheer on their favorite sports team, one thing is for certain: anything can happen!

ICE-CREAM PURR-LOR
ANTICS
Zzz...
ENJOYING A
LAZY SUNDAE

RIDING ON THE
MILKSHAKE MACHINE
SOAKING UP THE
SWEET LIFE

MEW YORK CITY ESCAPADES

SPEEDING DOWN THE ROLLER COASTERS AT CONEY ISLAND
CONEY ISLAND
AMUSEMENT PARK
ARCADE
CAUTION
May cause hair balls!

PLAYING HIDE-AND-SEEK IN CENTRAL PAWK

VACATION ADVENTURES

GETTING CARRIED AWAY IN HOT-AIR BALLOONS

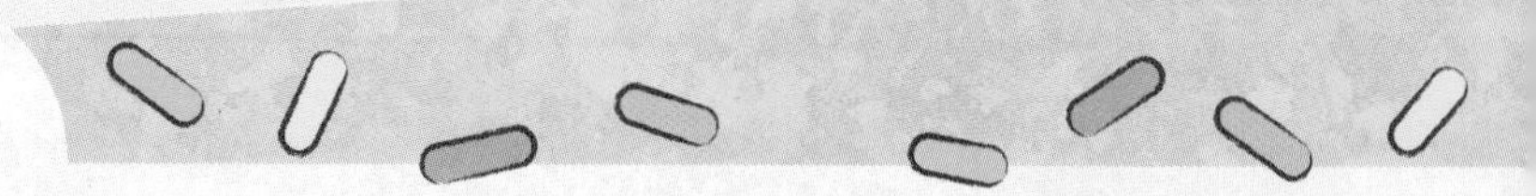

HEADING TO THE
WILDBERRY WEST
Hi-Yo
Coney.
AWAY!

OUT-OF-THIS WORLD ADVENTURE

BLASTING THROUGH THE MILKY WAY

SEARCHING FOR
DEEP-SEA TREASURE

THE SWEETEST TREASURE IN THE SEA

A KITTY CONES TAIL

"Arrr, me kitties," Blackbarry said one day. "I've gotten wind there be a priceless treasure hidden beneath the **BAY OF BENGAL CAT**."

"A treasure!" exclaimed Koko. "What is it?"

"Is it as rare as jewels?" asked Uma.

"As tasty as an orange?" asked Sherburt. His friends all looked at him. "What?" Sherburt asked. "That sounds like a **FRUITFUL TREASURE** to me!"

"It be the sweetest treasure under the sea," said Blackbarry. "But the waters of Bengal Cat Bay be feisty, and the journey deep. What say ye, me hearties? Be you up for the challenge?"

The Kitty Cones all grinned. "***FUR*** **SURE**!"

Soon, they were all deep-sea diving in their cones down to the bottom of the black, black waters of the Bay of Bengal Cat.

"I can't see anything," complained Sourpuss.

"Uma, can you help light our way?" asked Miyu.

"Of course!" Uma exclaimed. With a sprinkle of twinkles, Uma magically made her rainbow cone light up as bright as a shooting star.

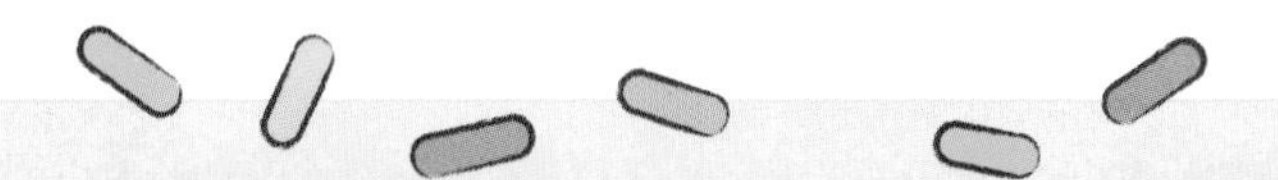

Now the Kitty Cones could see everything: the plants, the fish . . . and a cat shark heading straight for them!

"Quick, hide under your cones!" cried Yumi.

With a whisk and a whirl, the Kitty Cones zipped under their cones. The cat shark passed right by. It never even saw them!

"Whew, talk about being saved by the cone!" said Koko.

"And yaaarrr, there be the treasure!" cried Blackbarry.

Blackbarry pointed to the ruins of a shipwreck where a large treasure chest was nestled.

Quickly, the friends swam up to it. They each held their breath.

Blackbarry opened the lid to find . . .

"Coins!" cried all the Kitty Cones. "Lots and lots of golden coins!"

"And not just any coins," said Blackbarry. "Golden-wrapped chocolate coins!"

The Kitty Cones gasped.

"Chocolate coins!" cried Koko. "I love chocolate coins!"

"This is way better than an orange!" Sherburt said.

"I told ye." Blackbarry winked. "This be the sweetest treasure under the sea."

WHAT KITTY CONES LIKE

READING

KITTY CONES' TOP TEN FAVORITE BOOKS

1. GOODNIGHT MEW-N

2. EVERYONE SCOOPS

3. ROMEOW AND JULIET

4. THE BERRY HUNGRY KITTY CONE

5. MEOWTHER GOOSE'S FURR-Y TAILS

6. THE LITTLE PAWPRINTS

7. THE GREAT CATSBY

8. THE WIZARD OF PAWZ

9. LITTLE MEOWS ON THE PURR-Y

10. JUNIE B. CONES

WATCHING KITTY CONES' TOP TEN

1. WILLY WHISKERS AND THE ICE-CREAM FACTORY

2. SPIDER-CAT: FAR FROM CONE

3. MISSION IM-PAW-SIBLE
4. PURR-ASIC WORLD
5. PAW WARS EPISODE MEW: ATTACK OF THE CONES

MEWVIES

FAVORITE FLICKS

6. THE LITTLE PURR-MAID

7. HAIRY PAW-TER AND THE SAUCERER'S CONE

8. HOW TO TRAIN YOUR KITTEN

9. THE AVENGE-PURRS

10. FUR-OZEN

LISTENING TO MEWSIC

MEW YORK CITY'S TOP TEN SONGS OF THE WEEK

1. "WELCOME TO MEW YORK" BY TAIL-OR SWIFT

2. "A MEOW-MENT LIKE THIS" BY CANDY CLAW-KSON

3. "PURR-T OF ME" BY KITTY PURRY

4. "PURR-ZERK" BY M+M

5. "THANK U, CATS"

BY ARIANA GATO

6. "TALKING TO THE MEW-N"

BY BRUNO MARS BAR

7. "CAN'T STOP THE FELINE"

BY JUSTIN TIMBERCAKE

8. "HIGH HOPS"

BY PANIC! AT THE COOKIE DOUGH

9. "WHEN YOU LOOK ME IN THE WHISKERS"

BY THE JONAS LITTER

10. "PURR-TY IN THE MEW.S.A."

BY MEWLY CYRUS

One day, Hayao was feeling a little down.

"What's wrong?" Purrstachio asked.

"I'm feeling homesick," Hayao admitted. "Sometimes I really miss Kittyoto City."

"I can help," said Purrstachio. "You just need to find your inner chill. Follow me!"

Purrstachio took Hayao to her favorite meditation spot overlooking Mew York City Bay. "Just hang upside down from the pier by your tail and *breathe*," she instructed. "Pretend you're a sail blowing in the breeze. How do you feel?"

"Still homesick," Hayao said. "And now a little seasick, too . . ."

"Not to worry," said Purrstachio, flipping down to the ground. "Let's try some meditation. It's sure to have you *feline* fine in no time."

Together, Purrstachio and Hayao stretched out on some mats. Purrstachio told Hayao to close his eyes.

"Tell me what you see," Purrstachio said.

"I see . . . Kittyoto City," said Hayao.

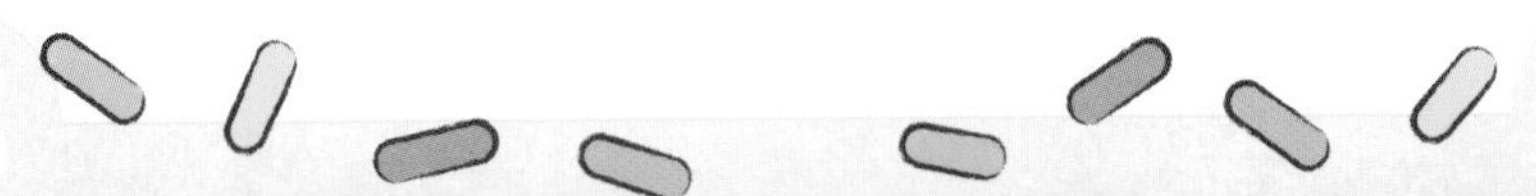

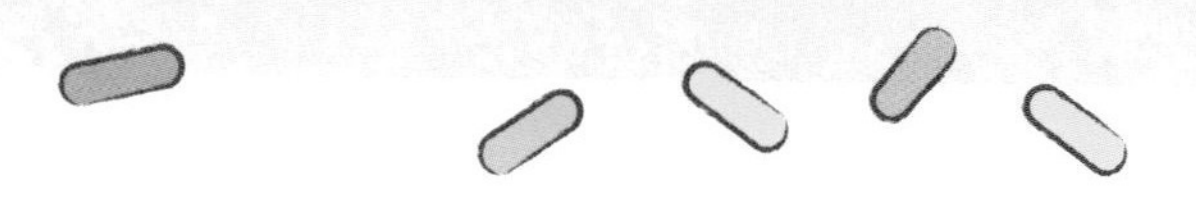

"Now imagine you're there," said Purrstachio. "Imagine you're surrounded by your friends, visiting your favorite spots."

"But my friends have never been to Kittyoto City," said Hayao. He opened his eyes. "Now I miss Kittyoto City *and* I want to bring my friends there!"

"Hmmmmm," said Purrstachio. "This is a little trickier than I thought. But I'm not giving up. When I'm feeling un-zen, I always turn to my favorite kitty guru, Dr. Chill. His show is full of scoops of wisdom!"

Together, the friends headed back to the ice-cream *purr*-lor. Purrstachio turned on the television. A Japanese cartoon popped up immediately.

"Hey, this is my favorite anime!" Hayao exclaimed. "*Astro Cat*! I love watching this show, especially with my friends. It reminds me that I can have a little bit of both my homes in the same place!"

The two kitties curled up to watch together.

"So you're feeling better?" Purrstachio asked.

"Yup!" said Hayao. "Thanks for helping me find my inner chill."

Purrstachio smiled. "What are friends for?"

FUN AND GAMES

SHERBURT'S COMEDY

Q: WHY DID THE KITTY CONE BUY THE NEWSPAPER?

A: SHE WANTED TO GET THE LATEST SCOOP.

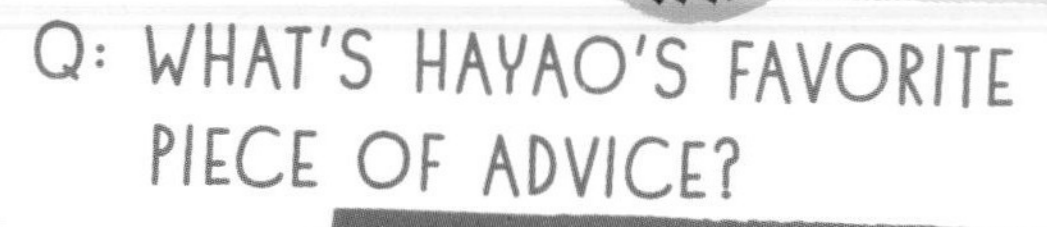

Q: WHAT'S HAYAO'S FAVORITE PIECE OF ADVICE?

A: DOUGH OR DOUGHNUT. THERE IS NO FRY.

Q: WHAT DID YUMI SAY TO MIYU WHEN THE SHOP RAN OUT OF VANILLA ICE-CREAM?

A: YOU'VE GOT TO BE KITTEN ME!

CORNER

Q: WHAT'S BLACKBARRY'S FAVORITE ICE-CREAM TOPPING?

A: SEA SALT COOKIE CRUMBLES

Q: WHAT DID THE KITTY CONES SAY TO SHERBURT ON HIS BIRTHDAY?

A: IT'S SHER-BURTDAY!

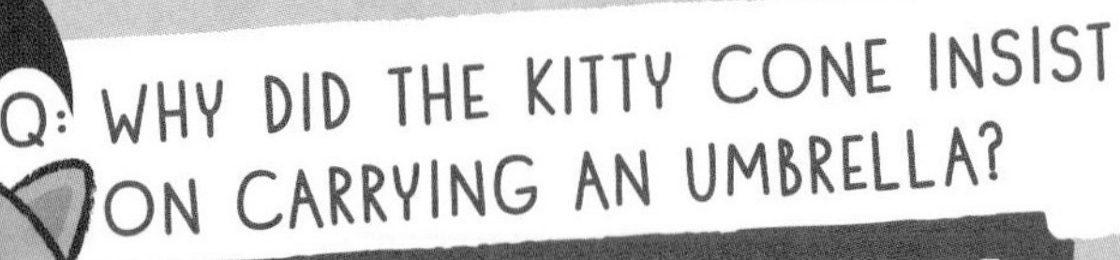

Q: WHY DID THE KITTY CONE INSIST ON CARRYING AN UMBRELLA?

A: THERE WAS A CHANCE OF SPRINKLES.

Q: HOW IS MIYU ALWAYS ABLE TO GET HER WAY?

A: SHE'S VERY *PURR*-SUASIVE!

Q: WHAT SOUND DOES A KITTY CONE MAKE WHEN SHE POPS HER GUM?

A: *CAT*-SPLAT!

Q: WHY DOES YUMI INSIST ON CARAMEL FOR HER ICE-CREAM WHEN EVERYONE ELSE ORDERS SPRINKLES?

A: SHE LIKES TO FEEL SAUCY.

Q: WHY DOESN'T CHIP LIKE SCI-FI MOVIES?

A: HE'S AFRAID OF SPACE-*CHIPS*.

Q: WHAT DID THE KITTY CONE SAY ABOUT THE ICE-CREAM SANDWICH?

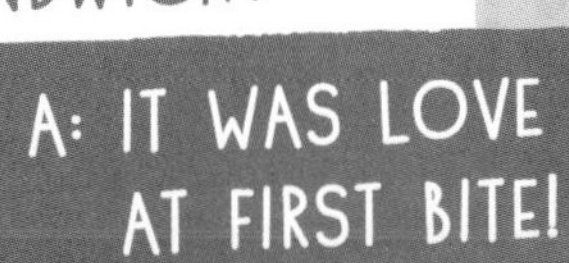

A: IT WAS LOVE AT FIRST BITE!

Q: IF KITTY CONES WERE PIGGY CONES, WHAT KIND OF ICE CREAM WOULD THEY EAT?

A: *HOGGIN*-DAZ

Q: WHAT WEIGHS MORE, A TON OF ICE-CREAM OR A TON OF KITTENS?

A: NEITHER, THEY BOTH WEIGH A TON!

Q: WHAT KIND OF MARKETS DO MIYU, KOKO, AND YUMI LIKE TO AVOID?

A: FLEA MARKETS.

SCOOPS OF WISDOM

FRIENDS BUILD EACH OTHER UP!

SPRINKLES
ATTRACT BIRDS.
TRUST US.

KEEP IT FLAVORFUL.

A BEST FRIEND STAYS WITH YOU LIKE A PAW PRINT ON YOUR HEART.

KEEP IT SWEET!

Thanks for hanging out with the Kitty Cones! They hope you had as sweet of a time meeting them as they did meeting you. And if you're ever in Mew York City, don't be a shy kitty. Drop on by for a fresh scoop and a **SPOONFUL OF FRIENDSHIP**. But don't be surprised if an out-of-this-world adventure pops up while you're there. Because when you're scooping up adventure together, **THE SKY'S THE LIMIT!**

SWEET!
ASTRO CAT

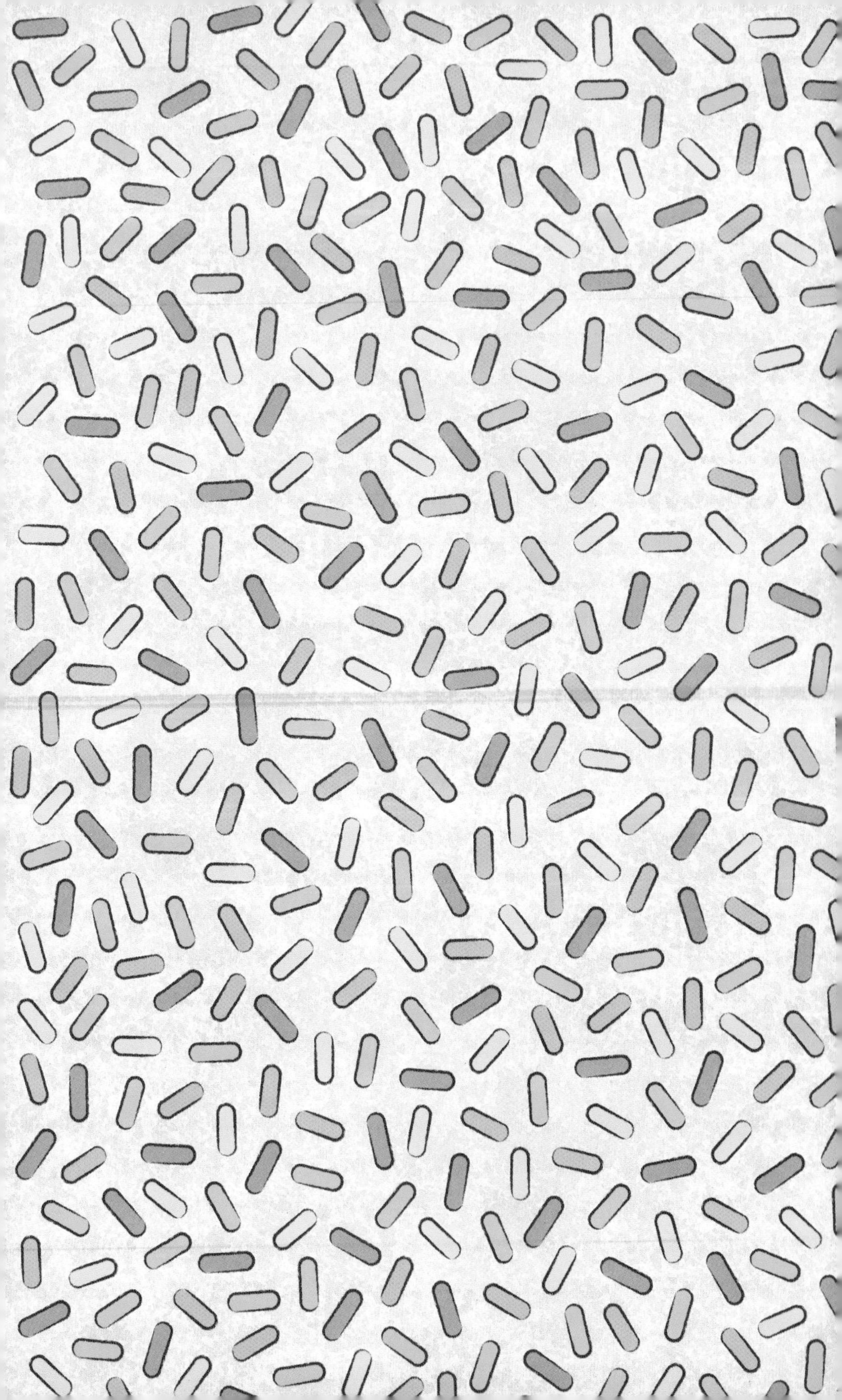

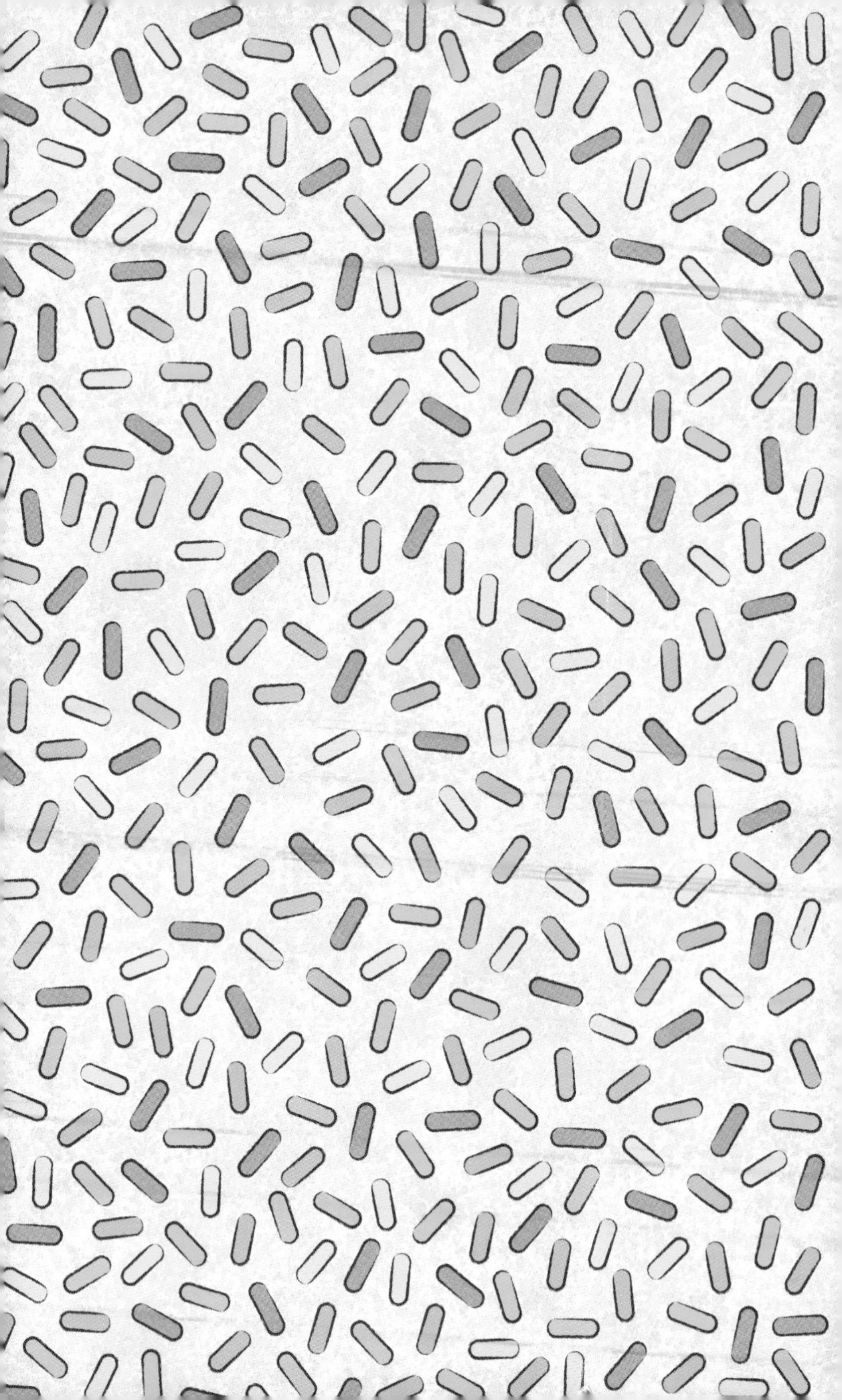

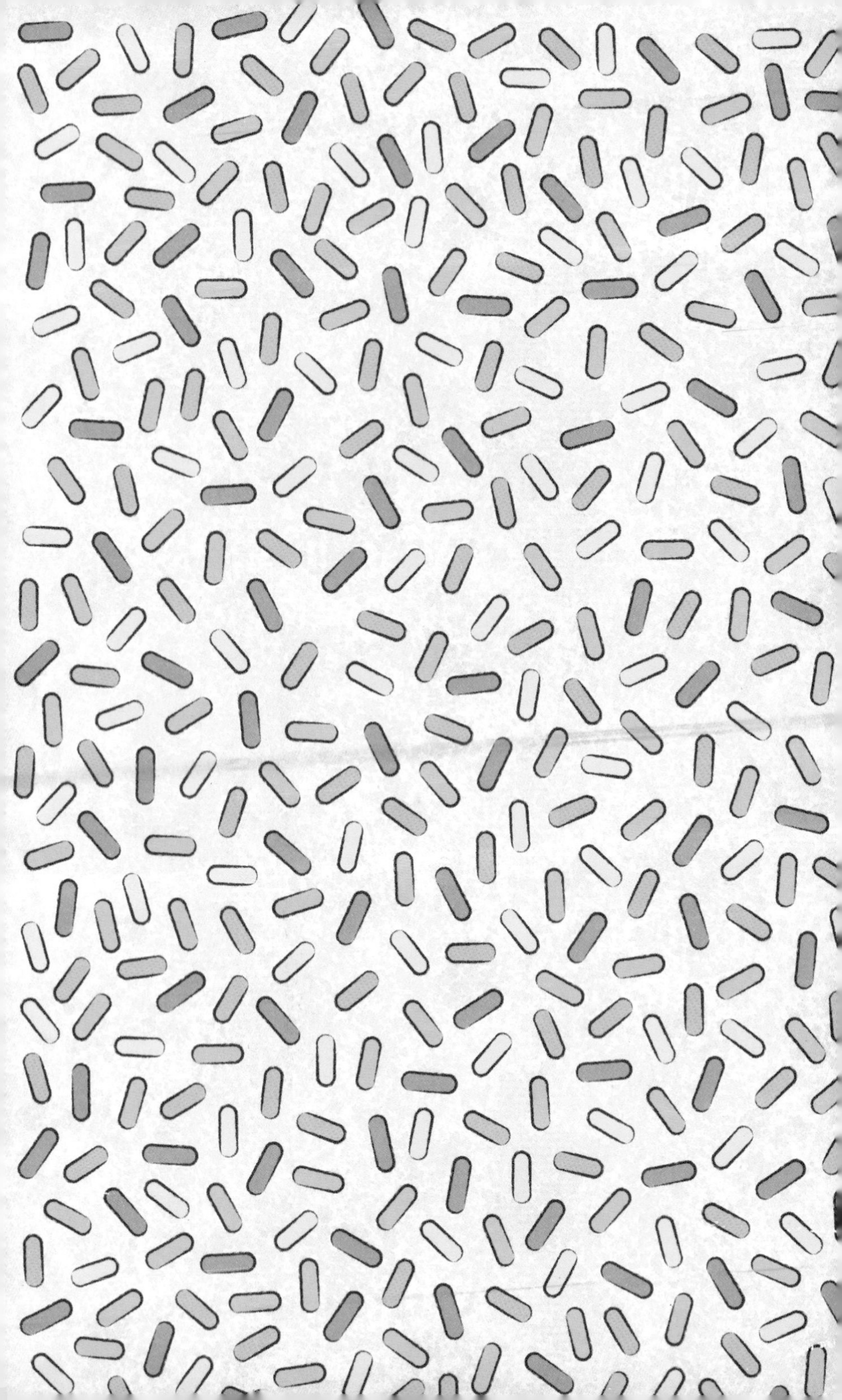